This book belongs to:

_____

 withdrawn form

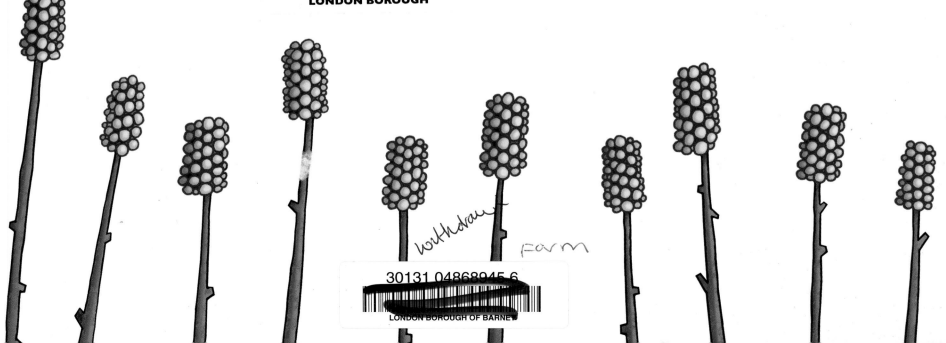

For Jake and Luke.

First published in Great Britain in 2011 by Andersen Press Ltd.,
20 Vauxhall Bridge Road, London SW1V 2SA.
Published in Australia by Random House Australia Pty,
Level 3, 100 Pacific Highway, North Sydney, NSW 2060.
Copyright © Mat Head, 2011.
The rights of Mat Head to be identified as the author and illustrator
of this work have been asserted by him in accordance with
the Copyright, Designs and Patents Act, 1988.
All rights reserved.
Colour separated in Switzerland by Photolitho AG, Zürich.
Printed and bound in Singapore by Tien Wah Press.
To create the artwork for this book Mat Head has hand drawn in
black & white line, scanned, coloured and then rendered in Photoshop.
10 9 8 7 6 5 4 3 2 1
British Library Cataloguing in Publication Data available.
ISBN 978 1 84939 198 6 (hbk)
ISBN 978 1 84939 226 6 (pbk)
This book has been printed on acid-free paper

P.Y.O. SWEETCORN

Mat Head

Warduff

and the corncob caper

ANDERSEN PRESS

Warduff was having a snooze.
Apart from the snoring – and an occasional fishy burp –
it had been a peaceful evening in the town.

Absolutely no dramas of any description whatsoever . . .

WARNING!

DO NOT APPROACH

Ring, ring.

Ring, ring.

ring.

"FOX ALERT! FOX ALERT!"
It was Fefferflap from Corncob Farm and she was in a pickle.
"WARDUFF, WARDUFF,
please come quickly!
There's a fox, and he's coming
round for tea, and
the trouble is . . .

I THINK
WE'RE ON
THE MENU!"

"Right," said Warduff, "keep your feathers on. I'm on my way."

When Warduff reached the farm, all the
animals were waiting for him,

"WARDUFF! PLEASE SAVE US! WE DON'T WANT TO DIE!"

They seemed a little tense.

"Now calm down, everyone," said Warduff. "Let's not panic. What's called for here is a plan. If you need me, I'll be over in the fields, thinking of one."

So Warduff wandered. And pondered.
Up a path. Down a track.

Further into the fields.
Deeper into his thoughts.

And then it hit him.

An absolutely **brilliant** idea.

Warduff went straight back to the others.
It was time to explain his plans for the night ahead.

And before long, Operation Corncob was underway.

Meanwhile, high above the farm, a shady figure paused for a moment, sniffed the air and smacked his chops.

Snipe also had plans for the night ahead.

He slid silently down the slope and into the farmyard.
Suddenly, there was a shuffle in the shadows, a light
flashed on and there, frozen in the glare, was Geoffrey . . .

. . . a rather tasty-looking dormouse.

"You must be supper!" grinned Snipe, edging closer.

But then, just as Snipe was about to pounce, Geoffrey's little legs came to life and he shot off into the fields.

"Oh, I do love a chase!" smirked Snipe, as he followed the footprints into the gloom.

Deeper and darker went the trail, then suddenly . . .

. . . the tracks stopped.
They just stopped.

What was going on?
Where on earth was that dormouse?
And why did Snipe suddenly feel
like someone was watching him?

"BE QUIET!"

roared the creature. "I am Gronklenork – the biggest, baddest monster of them all, and this is the bit where **you** get MUNCHED!"

But Snipe had already scarpered.

Come to think of it, Gronklenork had disappeared too.
But Geoffrey was there. And Warduff and Fefferflap.
In fact everyone was there, each holding their corncobs and
all laughing their heads off at how they had tricked Snipe.

Hooray for Warduff and his brilliant plan!

And so the celebrations began.

"Oh, you shouldn't have," said Warduff as a giant fish cake appeared, "but I'm so glad you did!"

"We just wanted to thank you for helping us," said the animals. "It's what friends are for," said Warduff.

And if you've got friends like that, you usually get a happy ending.

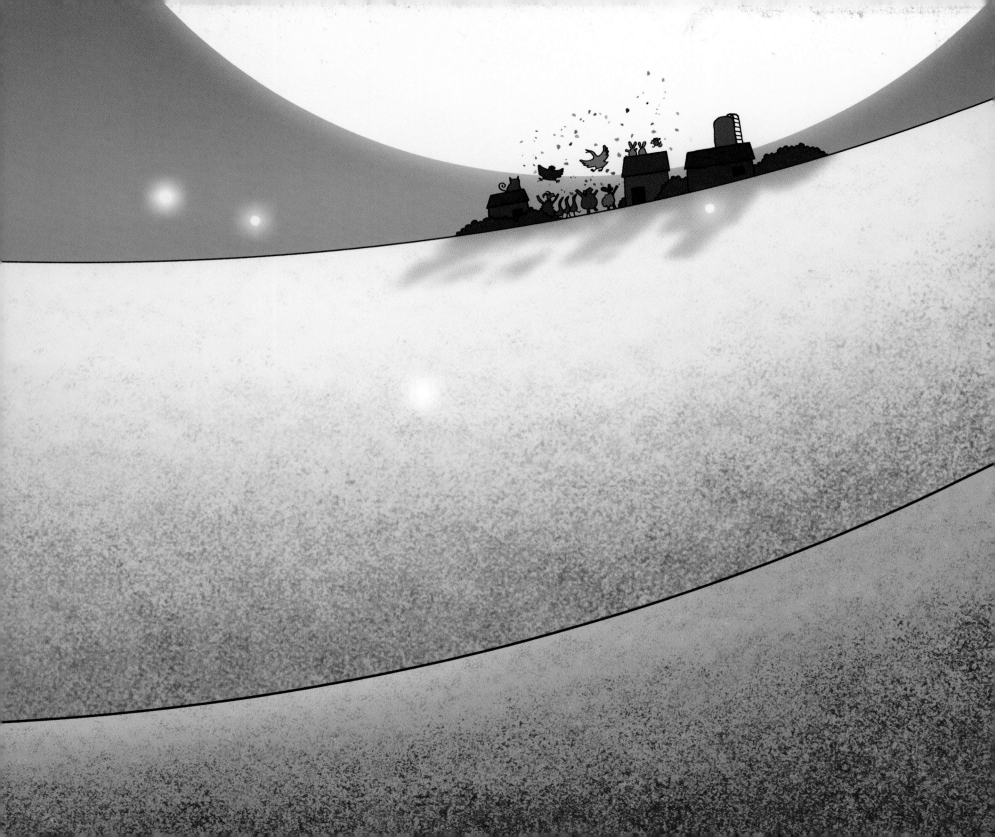

Other books you might enjoy:

WHO'S IN THE LOO?

by Jeanne Willis and Adrian Reynolds

9781842706985

THE TALENT SHOW

by Jo Hodgkinson

9781849390767

WHEN I WOKE UP I WAS A HIPPOPOTAMUS

by Tom MacRae and Ross Collins

9781849393591

JEREMIAH JELLYFISH FLIES HIGH!

by John Fardell

9781849391474

FORTUNATELY, UNFORTUNATELY

by Michael Foreman

9781849392242